'Twas the Night Before
CHRISTMAS
and Other Seasonal Favorites

THE METROPOLITAN MUSEUM OF ART
HARRY N. ABRAMS, INC., PUBLISHERS • NEW YORK

All of the works of art reproduced in this book are from the collections of The Metropolitan Museum of Art.

FRONT COVER: *It Must Be St. Nick.* Arthur Rackham, British, 1867–1939. From *The Night Before Christmas,* published in Philadelphia, 1931. Commercial color process, 5½ x 4 in. Gift of Mrs. John Barry Ryan, transferred from the Library 1983.1223.9

FRONT FLAP: *Santa Claus in His Sleigh.* American, ca. 1880–1905. Advertising card for Union Pacific Tea Co. Chromolithograph. The Jefferson R. Burdick Collection, Gift of Jefferson R. Burdick, 1947

ENDPAPERS: Back cover illustration from *The Mysterious Toyshop, A Fairy Tale.* Wyndham Payne, British, active 1920–30. Published in London, 1924. Color woodcut, 9 x 5⅛ in. Rogers Fund, 1970   1970.544.1

TITLE PAGE: *A Winter Carnival in a Small Flemish Town.* Peeter Gysels, Flemish, 1621–1690/91. Oil on copper, 10¼ x 13¼ in. Gift of Francis Neilson, 1945   45.146.4

CONTENTS PAGE: *Wreath with Santa Claus.* American, early 20th century. Color lithograph, Diam. 3½ in. The Jefferson R. Burdick Collection, Gift of Jefferson R. Burdick, 1947   album 525, p. 8

BACK FLAP: *Santa Claus with Plum Puddings.* American, ca. 1880–1905. Advertising card for Atmore's Mince Meat and Genuine English Plum Pudding. Chromolithograph, published by Ketterlinus, Philadelphia. The Jefferson R. Burdick Collection, Gift of Jefferson R. Burdick, 1947

BACK COVER: *Santa Claus Making a Sled.* American, ca. 1912. Color lithograph, 5⅛ x 3⅛ in. The Jefferson R. Burdick Collection, Gift of Jefferson R. Burdick, 1947   album 457, p. 22 recto

Published in 2003 by The Metropolitan Museum of Art, New York, and Harry N. Abrams, Incorporated, New York.
Copyright © 2003 by The Metropolitan Museum of Art

First Edition
Printed in Hong Kong
12 11 10 09 08 07 06 05 04 03   5 4 3 2 1

Produced by the Department of Special Publications, The Metropolitan Museum of Art: Robie Rogge, Publishing Manager; William Lach, Project Editor; Anna Raff, Designer. All photography by The Metropolitan Museum of Art Photograph Studio.

Visit the Museum's Web site: www.metmuseum.org

Library of Congress Cataloging-in-Publication Data

'Twas the night before Christmas, and other seasonal favorites.
      p. cm.
   ISBN 1-58839-082-9 (MMA).—ISBN 0-8109-4592-4 (Abrams).
   1. Christmas—Poetry. 2. American poetry. 3. English poetry. I. Metropolitan Museum of Art (New York, N.Y.)
PS595.C48T88 2003
811.008'0334—dc21

Harry N. Abrams, Inc.
100 Fifth Avenue
New York, NY 10011
www.abramsbooks.com

Abrams is a subsidiary of

LA MARTINIÈRE
GROUPE

CONTENTS

INTRODUCTION

There are many Christmases. There is the family Christmas of gifts and decorated firs, the fairy-tale Christmas of Santa and the reindeer, the ancient Christmas of winter and light, and the spiritual Christmas of Christ in the manger. With so many ways to celebrate, and with so much anticipation, indulgence, and introspection around these celebrations, December 25 always seems to last at least as long as the twelve days of the old carol.

This collection of poetry and art from The Metropolitan Museum of Art attempts to gather much of the holiday season's bounty, from the rollicking to the reverent. An American greeting card featuring children cavorting in the snow captures the anticipation of "In the Week When Christmas Comes," by English lyricist Eleanor Farjeon. Arthur Rackham's classic illustrations of Santa Claus embody Clement C. Moore's beloved Old Saint Nick. A Russian storybook Snow Queen matches the dreamlike voice of "Velvet Shoes," by American poet Elinor Wylie. And a medieval stained-glass window reflects the forceful imagery of "Star of the Nativity," by twentieth-century Nobel laureate Joseph Brodsky.

Each Yuletide, no matter how you celebrate, open this book and let the work of artists and poets, famous or forgotten, from past or present, wish you the merriest of Christmases and the happiest of New Years.

—William Lach

Lune. Lucien Laforge, French, 1889–?
From an alphabet book published by Henry Goulet, Paris, ca. 1925. Woodcut, printed in colors.
Harris Brisbane Dick Fund, 1930   30.96.7 leaf L

The Shepherds and the Angels

Luke 2:8–14

And there were in the same country shepherds abiding in the
field, keeping watch over their flock by night.

And, lo, the angel of the Lord came upon them, and the glory of
the Lord shone round about them; and they were sore afraid.

And the angel said unto them, Fear not: for, behold, I bring you
good tidings of great joy, which shall be to all people.

For unto you is born this day in the city of David a Saviour,
which is Christ the Lord.

And this shall be a sign unto you; Ye shall find the babe
wrapped in swaddling clothes, lying in a manger.

And suddenly there was with the angel a multitude of the
heavenly host praising God, and saying,

> Glory to God in the highest,
> and on earth peace,
> good will toward men.

The Annunciation to the Shepherds (detail). Henri Rivière, French, 1864–1951.
From a broadside for the book *La Marche à l'étoile* by Georges Fragerolle. Color lithograph, 11⅛ x 16 in.
The Elisha Whittelsey Collection, The Elisha Whittelsey Fund, 1966 66.559.65

Simple Gifts

Joseph Brackett, American, 1797–1882

'Tis the gift to be simple,
'Tis the gift to be free,
'Tis the gift to come down
Where we ought to be,
And when we find ourselves in the place just right,
'Twill be in the valley of love and delight.

When true simplicity is gain'd,
To bow and to bend we shan't be asham'd,
To turn, turn will be our delight
'Til by turning, turning we come round right.

I Saw Three Ships

English carol

I saw three ships come sailing in,
Come sailing in, come sailing in.
I saw three ships come sailing in
On Christmas Day in the morning.

And what do you think was in them then,
Was in them then, was in them then?
And what do you think was in them then
On Christmas Day in the morning?

Three pretty girls were in them then,
Were in them then, were in them then.
Three pretty girls were in them then
On Christmas Day in the morning.

And one could whistle and one could sing
And one could play on the violin,
Such joy there was at my wedding
On Christmas Day in the morning.

Star of the Nativity

Joseph Brodsky, American, 1940–1996

In the cold season, in a locality accustomed to heat more than
to cold, to horizontality more than to a mountain,
a child was born in a cave in order to save the world;
it blew as only in deserts in winter it blows, athwart.

To Him, all things seemed enormous: His mother's breast, the steam
out of the ox's nostrils, Caspar, Balthazar, Melchior—the team
of Magi, their presents heaped by the door, ajar.
He was but a dot, and a dot was the star.

Keenly, without blinking, through pallid, stray
clouds, upon the child in the manger, from far away—
from the depth of the universe, from its opposite end—the star
was looking into the cave. And that was the Father's stare.

In the Week When Christmas Comes

Eleanor Farjeon, English, 1881–1965

This is the week when Christmas comes.
Let every pudding burst with plums,
And every tree bear dolls and drums,
In the week when Christmas comes.

Let every hall have boughs of green,
With berries glowing in between,
In the week when Christmas comes.

Let every doorstep have a song,
Sounding the dark street along,
In the week when Christmas comes.

Let every steeple ring a bell,
With a joyful tale to tell,
In the week when Christmas comes.

Let every night put forth a star,
To show us where the heavens are,
In the week when Christmas comes.

Let every stable have a lamb,
Sleeping warm beside its dam,
In the week when Christmas comes.

This is the week when Christmas comes.

The Season's Greetings. Corwin Knapp Linson, American, 1864–1959.
Color lithograph, 4 x 6 in., early 20th century. The Jefferson R. Burdick Collection,
Gift of Jefferson R. Burdick, 1947   album 525, p.36

A. Varin del et sc.

G. de Gonet édit.

Christmas-Greetings

Lewis Carroll, English, 1832–1898

from a fairy to a child

Lady, dear, if Fairies may
    For a moment lay aside
Cunning tricks and elfish play,
    'Tis at happy Christmas-tide.

We have heard the children say—
    Gentle children, whom we love—
Long ago, on Christmas Day,
    Came a message from above.

Still, as Christmas-tide comes round,
    They remember it again—
Echo still the joyful sound
    "Peace on earth, good-will to men!"

Yet the hearts must childlike be
    Where such heavenly guests abide;
Unto children, in their glee,
    All the year is Christmas-tide!

Thus, forgetting tricks and play
    For a moment, Lady dear,
We would wish you, if we may,
    Merry Christmas, glad New Year!

L'Arbre de Noël. Amédée Varin, French, 1818–1883.
Illustration for *Les Papillons*, published in Paris, 1852. Steel or wood engraving, hand-colored, 10⅞ x 8¼ in.
Gift of Lincoln Kirstein, 1970   1970.565.31

from The Friendly Beasts

English carol

Jesus our brother, strong and good,
Was humbly born in a stable rude,
And the friendly beasts around Him stood,
Jesus our brother, strong and good.

"I," said the donkey, all gray and brown,
"I carried His mother up hill and down;
I carried her safely to Bethlehem town."
"I," said the donkey, all gray and brown.

"I," said the cow, all tan and red,
"I gave Him my manger for His bed;
I gave Him my hay to pillow His head."
"I," said the cow, all tan and red.

"I," said the sheep with curly horn,
"I gave Him my wool for His blanket warm;
He wore my coat on Christmas morn."
"I," said the sheep with curly horn.

Thus every beast by some good spell,
In the stable dark was glad to tell
Of the gift he gave Immanuel,
The gift he gave Immanuel.

The Nativity (detail). German, third quarter 15th century.
Altar frontal with scenes from the life of the Virgin. Wool, silk, and metal thread on linen warp, 3 ft. 5 in. x 11 ft. 6 in.
Gift of Charles F. Iklé, 1957   57.126

'Twas the Night Before Christmas

Clement C. Moore, American, 1779–1863

'Twas the night before Christmas, when all through the house

Not a creature was stirring, not even a mouse;

The stockings were hung by the chimney with care,

In hopes that St. Nicholas soon would be there;

The children were nestled all snug in their beds,

While visions of sugar-plums danced in their heads;

And Mamma in her kerchief, and I in my cap,

Had just settled our brains for a long winter's nap,

When out on the lawn there arose such a clatter,

I sprang from the bed to see what was the matter.

Away to the window I flew like a flash,

Tore open the shutters and threw up the sash.

The moon on the breast of the new-fallen snow

Gave the lustre of midday to objects below,

When, what to my wondering eyes should appear,

But a miniature sleigh, and eight tiny reindeer,

With a little old driver, so lively and quick,

I knew in a moment it must be St. Nick.

More rapid than eagles his coursers they came,

And he whistled, and shouted, and called them by name:

"Now, Dasher! now, Dancer! now, Prancer and Vixen!

On, Comet! on, Cupid! on, Donner and Blitzen!

To the top of the porch! to the top of the wall!

Now dash away! dash away! dash away all!"

As dry leaves that before the wild hurricane fly,

When they meet with an obstacle, mount to the sky,

So up to the house-top the coursers they flew,

With the sleigh full of toys, and St. Nicholas too.

The Children Were Nestled All Snug in Their Beds. Arthur Rackham, British, 1867–1939.
From *The Night Before Christmas*, published in Philadelphia, 1931. Commercial color process, 5½ x 4 in.
Gift of Mrs. John Barry Ryan, transferred from the Library   1983.1223.9

And then, in a twinkling, I heard on the roof

The prancing and pawing of each little hoof.

As I drew in my head, and was turning around,

Down the chimney St. Nicholas came with a bound.

He was dressed all in fur, from his head to his foot,

And his clothes were all tarnished with ashes and soot;

A bundle of toys he had flung on his back,

And he looked like a pedlar just opening his pack.

His eyes—how they twinkled! his dimples how merry!

His cheeks were like roses, his nose like a cherry!

His droll little mouth was drawn up like a bow,

And the beard of his chin was as white as the snow;

The stump of a pipe he held tight in his teeth,

And the smoke it encircled his head like a wreath;

He had a broad face and a little round belly,

That shook when he laughed, like a bowlful of jelly.

He was chubby and plump, a right jolly old elf,

And I laughed when I saw him, in spite of myself;

A wink of his eye and a twist of his head

Soon gave me to know I had nothing to dread.

He spoke not a word, but went straight to his work,

And filled all the stockings; then turned with a jerk,

And laying a finger aside of his nose,

And giving a nod, up the chimney he rose;

He sprang to his sleigh, to his team gave a whistle,

And away they all flew like the down of a thistle.

But I heard him exclaim, ere he drove out of sight,

"Happy Christmas to all and to all a good night!"

And Giving a Nod, Up the Chimney He Rose. Arthur Rackham, British, 1867–1939.
From *The Night Before Christmas*, published in Philadelphia, 1931. Commercial color process, 5¼ x 4 in.
Gift of Mrs. John Barry Ryan, transferred from the Library 1983.1223.9

from Christmas Bells

Henry Wadsworth Longfellow, American, 1807–1882

I heard the bells on Christmas Day
Their old familiar carols play,
And wild and sweet
The words repeat
Of peace on earth, good-will to men!

And in despair I bowed my head;
"There is no peace on earth," I said,
"For hate is strong
And mocks the song
Of peace on earth, good-will to men!"

Then pealed the bells more loud and deep:
"God is not dead, nor doth he sleep;
The wrong shall fail,
The right prevail,
With peace on earth, good-will to men!"

Till ringing, singing on its way,
The world revolved from night to day,
A voice, a chime,
A chant sublime,
Of peace on earth, good-will to men!

Christmas Eve Church. Jeanne Kerremans, Belgian, active 1930s.
From *Le Manteau du Roi et autres contes de Noël* by Camille Melloy, published in Brussels, 1939.
Color lithograph, 6⅛ x 6⅛ in. Gift of C. Whitney Dall Jr., in memory of Emily M. Dall, 1976   1976.625.3

Carol of the Brown King

Langston Hughes, American, 1902–1967

Of the three Wise Men
Who came to the King,
One was a brown man,
So they sing.

Of the three Wise Men
Who followed the Star,
One was a brown king
From afar.

They brought fine gifts
Of spices and gold
In jeweled boxes
Of beauty untold.

Unto His humble
Manger they came
And bowed their heads
In Jesus' name.

Three Wise Men,
One dark like me—
Part of His
Nativity.

The Adoration of the Magi (detail). Workshop of Gerard David, Flemish, born about 1455, died 1523. Oil on wood, 27½ x 28⅞ in. The Jack and Belle Linsky Collection, 1982   1982.60.17

Little Tree

E. E. Cummings, American, 1894–1962

little tree
little silent Christmas tree
you are so little
you are more like a flower

who found you in the green forest
and were you very sorry to come away?
see   i will comfort you
because you smell so sweetly

i will kiss your cool bark
and hug you safe and tight
just as your mother would,
only don't be afraid

look   the spangles
that sleep all the year in a dark box
dreaming of being taken out and allowed to shine,
the balls the chains red and gold the fluffy threads,

put up your little arms
and i'll give them all to you to hold
every finger shall have its ring
and there won't be a single place dark or unhappy

then when you're quite dressed
you'll stand in the window for everyone to see
and how they'll stare!
oh but you'll be very proud

and my little sister and i will take hands
and looking up at our beautiful tree
we'll dance and sing
"Noel Noel"

Children and Christmas Tree. Mela Koehler, Austrian, 1885–1960. Color lithograph, 5½ x 3½ in., ca. 1908–14. Museum Accession

from The Bells

Edgar Allan Poe, American, 1809–1849

Hear the sledges with the bells—
Silver bells!
What a world of merriment their melody foretells!
How they tinkle, tinkle, tinkle,
In the icy air of night!
While the stars that oversprinkle
All the Heavens, seem to twinkle
With a crystalline delight;
Keeping time, time, time,
In a sort of Runic rhyme,
To the tintinnabulation that so musically wells
From the bells, bells, bells, bells,
Bells, bells, bells—
From the jingling and the tinkling of the bells.

Rise Up, Shepherd, and Follow!

American spiritual

There's a star in the East on Christmas morn.
Rise up, shepherd, and follow!

It will lead to the place where the Savior's born.
Rise up, shepherd, and follow!

Leave your sheep and leave your lambs.
Rise up, shepherd, and follow!

Leave your ewes and leave your rams.
Rise up, shepherd, and follow!

Follow, follow!
Rise up, shepherd, and follow!

Follow the star of Bethlehem.
Rise up, shepherd, and follow!

The Block (detail). Romare Bearden, American, 1911–1988.
Cut and pasted papers on Masonite, 4 ft. x 18 ft., 1971. Gift of Mr. and Mrs. Samuel Shore, 1978   1978.61.2

Christmas Poem

Mary Oliver, American, b. 1935

Says a country legend told every year:
Go to the barn on Christmas Eve and see
what the creatures do as that long night tips over.
Down on their knees they will go, the fire
of an old memory whistling through their minds!

I went. Wrapped to my eyes against the cold
I creaked back the barn door and peered in.
From town the church bells spilled their midnight music,
and the beasts listened—
yet they lay in their stalls like stone.

Oh the heretics!
Not to remember Bethlehem,
or the star as bright as a sun,
or the child born on a bed of straw!
To know only of the dissolving Now!

Still they drowsed on—
citizens of the pure, the physical world,
they loomed in the dark: powerful
of body, peaceful of mind,
innocent of history.

The Farmland in Winter (detail). Published by Currier and Ives, American, 1857–1907.
Color lithograph, 16⅛ x 23¹¹/₁₆ in., 1861. Bequest of Adele S. Colgate, 1962   63.550.506

Brothers! I whispered. *It is Christmas!*
And you are no heretics, but a miracle,
immaculate still as when you thundered forth
on the morning of creation!
As for Bethlehem, that blazing star

still sailed the dark, but only looked for me.
Caught in its light, listening again to its story,
I curled against some sleepy beast, who nuzzled
my hair as though I were a child, and warmed me
the best it could all night.

Mistletoe

Walter de la Mare, English, 1873–1956

Sitting under the mistletoe
(Pale-green, fairy mistletoe),
One last candle burning low,
All the sleepy dancers gone,
Just one candle burning on,
Shadows lurking everywhere:
Someone came, and kissed me there.

Tired I was; my head would go
Nodding under the mistletoe
(Pale-green, fairy mistletoe);
No footsteps came, no voice, but only,
Just as I sat there, sleepy, lonely,
Stooped in the still and shadowy air
Lips unseen—and kissed me there.

from The Boy Who Laughed at Santa Claus

Ogden Nash, American, 1902–1971

In Baltimore there lived a boy.

He wasn't anybody's joy.

Although his name was Jabez Dawes,

His character was full of flaws.

In school he never led his classes,

He hid old ladies' reading glasses,

His mouth was open when he chewed,

And elbows to the table glued.

He stole the milk of hungry kittens,

And walked through doors marked NO ADMITTANCE.

He said he acted thus because

There wasn't any Santa Claus.…

The children wept all Christmas eve

And Jabez chortled up his sleeve.

No infant dared hang up his stocking

For fear of Jabez' ribald mocking.

He sprawled on his untidy bed,

Fresh malice dancing in his head,

When presently with scalp a-tingling,

Jabez heard a distant jingling;

He heard the crunch of sleigh and hoof

Crisply alighting on the roof.

What good to rise and bar the door?

A shower of soot was on the floor.

What was beheld by Jabez Dawes?

The fireplace full of Santa Claus!
Then Jabez fell upon his knees
With cries of "Don't," and "Pretty Please."
He howled, "I don't know where you read it,
But anyhow, I never said it!"
"Jabez," replied the angry saint,
"It isn't I, it's you that ain't.
Although there is a Santa Claus,
There isn't any Jabez Dawes!"
Said Jabez then with impudent vim,
"Oh, yes there is, and I am him!
Your magic don't scare me, it doesn't,"
And suddenly he found he wasn't!
From grimy feet to grimy locks,
Jabez became a Jack-in-the-box,
An ugly toy with springs unsprung,
Forever sticking out his tongue.
The neighbors heard his mournful squeal;
They searched for him, but not with zeal.
No trace was found of Jabez Dawes,
Which led to thunderous applause,
And people drank a loving cup
And went and hung their stockings up.
All you who sneer at Santa Claus,
Beware the fate of Jabez Dawes,
The saucy boy who mocked the saint.
Donner and Blitzen licked off his paint.

Filled All the Stockings. Arthur Rackham, British, 1867–1939.
From *The Night Before Christmas*, published in Philadelphia, 1931. Commercial color process, 5¼ x 4 in.
Gift of Mrs. John Barry Ryan, transferred from the Library   1983.1223.9

A Christmas Alphabet

Carolyn Wells, American, 1862–1942

A is for Angel who graces the tree.

B is for Bells that chime out in glee.

C is for Candle to light Christmas Eve.

D is for Dreams which we truly believe.

E is for Evergreens cut for the room.

F is for Flowers of exquisite perfume.

G is for Gifts that bring us delight.

H is for Holly with red berries bright.

I is for Ice, so shining and clear.

J is the Jingle of bells far and near.

K is Kriss Kringle with fur cap and coat.

L is for Letters the children all wrote.

M is for Mother, who's trimming the bough.

N is for Night, see the stars sparkling now.

O is for Ornaments, dazzling with light.

P for Plum Pudding that tasted just right.

Q the Quadrille, in which each one must dance.

R is for Reindeer that gallop and prance.

S is for Snow that falls silently down.

T is for Turkey, so tender and brown.

U is for Uproar that goes on all day.

V is for Voices that carol a lay.

W is for Wreaths hung up on the wall.

X is for Xmas, with pleasures for all.

Y is for Yule log that burns clear and bright.

Z is for Zest shown from morning till night.

Angel with Christmas Tree and Children. Published by Franz Huld, American, New York, ca. 1898.
Chromolithograph, 5¼ x 3¼ in. The Jefferson R. Burdick Collection, Gift of Jefferson R. Burdick, 1947   album 457, p. 11r

Velvet Shoes

Elinor Wylie, American, 1885–1928

Let us walk in the white snow
　　In a soundless space;
With footsteps quiet and slow,
　　At a tranquil pace,
　　Under veils of white lace.

I shall go shod in silk,
　　And you in wool,
White as a white cow's milk,
　　More beautiful
　　Than the breast of a gull.

We shall walk through the still town
　　In a windless peace;
We shall step upon white down,
　　Upon silver fleece,
　　Upon softer than these.

We shall walk in velvet shoes:
　　Wherever we go
Silence will fall like dews
　　On white silence below.
　　We shall walk in the snow.

The Snow Maiden. Boris Zvorykin, Russian, 1872–?
Illustration for "Snegurochka" ("The Snow Maiden") in *L'Oiseau de feu et d'autres contes populaires russes.* Gouache, metallic inks, and black ink, heightened with white, over graphite. Gift of Thomas H. Guinzburg, The Viking Press, 1979   1979.537.15

from In Memoriam

Alfred, Lord Tennyson, English, 1809–1892

Ring out, wild bells, to the wild sky,
    The flying cloud, the frosty light:
    The year is dying in the night;
Ring out, wild bells, and let him die.

Ring out the old, ring in the new,
    Ring, happy bells, across the snow:
    The year is going, let him go;
Ring out the false, ring in the true.

Ring out the grief that saps the mind,
    For those that here we see no more;
    Ring out the feud of rich and poor,
Ring in redress to all mankind.

Ring out the want, the care, the sin,
    The faithless coldness of the times;
    Ring out, ring out my mournful rhymes,
But ring the fuller minstrel in.

Ring in the valiant man and free,
    The larger heart, the kindlier hand
    Ring out the darkness of the land,
Ring in the Christ that is to be.

Ring! Christmas Bell. Published in London by Ernest Nister, German, 1842–1909.
Color lithograph, 3½ x 5½ in., ca. 1910.
The Jefferson R. Burdick Collection, Gift of Jefferson R. Burdick, 1947   album 457, p. 12r

CREDITS

Central Park, Winter. William Glackens, American, 1870–1938. Oil on canvas, 25 x 30 in., ca. 1905. George A. Hearn Fund, 1921   21.164